Silver Lining

- Bala Shiva

For

The eyes

That's reading this,

I don't like wasting pages.

But it seems to be the trend now.

My brain screamed at me that evening,

"*What's up?*" I asked.

Brain said,

"*Let's make Milk and honey Parody*".

"*I don't want to plagiarize*", I said.

"*You can write with your own words, like Freedom of speech, perspective, thoughts and stuff man*", It replied.

"*Still I can't just copy her concepts. Many of them are too erotic*", I said.

"*It is not copying when it is your opinion, & if you want to be family friendly with your words, then do that. STOP ARGUING, you are bored and got nothing to do, just write what you want to and ignore everything else*", Brain brainwashed me.

"*Okay then*" as I opened MS word.

PS: I'm not going to use or make fun of her work. I'll write my own lines connected to her work. You may not even find any similarities.

When you are broken,

Broken into a million pieces...

You will not hurt anyone.

As you spend all of your time,

Collecting your pieces.

- One who is broken.

She was a play toy,

He did anything and everything that's plausible.

She doubted his ambiguous actions,

But he was fulfilling himself.

It was nothing but an exercise to his ego.

No passion or compassion involved.

- Play toy.

Women these days are easily hacked,

As they allow too many *guests* to access them.

Soon or later,

They will report *"inaccessible"* to everyone.

But what really happened is,

"They lost track of finding their admin".

     - Need a higher self-evaluation update.

Shattered home,

Battered memories,

Pains from the past,

But as your DNA ever last,

You are nothing but vile to me.

- Unquenchable.

Life for the little bunny was hard,

It was being trampled by the big ones,

It couldn't get away.

It's too weak and frail.

                    - Familiar Monster.

She was supposed to cherish only her saving grace,

The almighty who gave her flesh & bones,

The one who fed her with blood & blessings.

Yet, she had fallen prey to the dark side of her existence.

She refused to let it go,

Of the being whom played a fairly small part on her life and left her astray.

- Not every dad is a hero.

He brought her a bouquet,

A bouquet full of Colourful flowers,

To distract her from his *"black and white"* intentions.

- Bouquet

She fell in love,

An inexplicable collection of emotions & hormones.

She fell in love,

To an abusive acquaintance, who is similar to her devil.

She fell in love,

Believing that *"Known devil is better than any unknown angel"*.

It's her devil's fault.

- Devil's daughter.

We all are capable of it,

The most desirable love from our loved
ones,

But like scorpions, we continue stinging one
another to stimulate it.

Causing more pain than passion,

We rarely revise our real love for one
another.

- Sting.

The words "*She*" & "*He*" depicts what many should understand.

That "*he*" can be a part of "*she*",

And "*She*" can be more than "*he*".

Neither should take one another for granted.

But these day,

Both of the equals have an unequal understanding.

Majority of "*She*",

Believes they are superior and "*he*" is nothing more than a "*silver lining*" to them.

- Not a silver lining.

The monsters in disguise trapped her,

With full of hatred and no regret,

Treated her in ways she wasn't meant to be.

Lust took its tyranny,

Leaving her in tears and fears.

But she is still dear to whom she held near,

They said it loud, she understood it clear.

She might be torn, but she is still terrific.

- Not the End.

We have more *"voids"* than there is *"infinity"*,

We have more *"chaos"* than there is *"unity"*,

We fill our *"voids"* with sadness and make ourselves a *"chaos"*,

Our needs are *"infinite"* which stops us *"unite"*.

- Infinite chaos.

Parenting, it's tricky these days for parents.

But never should their child beg them for love.

Life gets more tangled as the day goes,

That doesn't mean the basic deeds should be ignored.

- Provide.

The father and mother were at war,

The child was the warzone.

One claimed victory over the other,

Then fell the nuke called *"Divorce"*.

The warzone was designated *"Dead Inside"*,

- Scarred for life.

Still there are women who are valued only when,

1. They are inside another woman,

2. They are invisible to the outside world,

3. They have another life inside them.

They never get to live as they wish.

For they have only one life.

Shame on you, "*World*",

For you haven't let go of your old ways.

                                        - Deprived women.

We all are nothing but a grain of sand, on a sand dune.

One which is among uncountable other dunes,

Dunes that are collectively a des(s)ert called "*our world*".

We may sway alone or stay in clusters,

Life may seem pointless and tedious every now and then,

But we are a part of the world.

We all have the right to be here and find our own place and path.

Let nobody, even yourself to tell that you are "*not worthy*".

- Live.

Speak,

Speak volumes,

Make opinionated noises,

Raise your voice.

For those who supress you, surprise them
by walking away,

They are toxic to your purity.

And for those who care, be bare with them.

Reward them, for the cherished circle they
are to you.

You and your voice matter.

But make sure your voice is "*pure*" and not
"*toxic*".

                                    - Voice.

Amidst all the mishaps and misunderstandings,

Amidst all the pain and suffering,

Amidst all the joy and happiness,

Amidst all the dread and fear,

Amidst all the success and failures,

Amidst all the cherishing and choosing,

They have the god like power to create life inside them.

Which no man can ever do, but takes pride on.

- Goddess.

The value of love is determined by the person showing it,

Not in quantity, but in quality.

The Standard for love is set by "*Mother*".

- Love Standard.

You are fire to my frozen heart,

You are heaven to my inferno,

You are a gentle breeze to my endless summer,

Oh, you are the forbidden fruit.

One that I need & want but can't have,

"You are my dawn & dusk."

- Eternal enigma.

For every being there will be a stigma.

From what I know,

You are my stigma.

A scar that cannot be unseen and unfelt,

A pain & pleasure i could not resist.

- Stigma.

Why has the world been cruel to me?

All I want is someone who slides his fingers into mine, Squeeze and holds my hands,.

Stare into my eyes,

And say something without any words,

Mean something without any menace,

Smile at me without any care.

Is wanting that unfair?

- Prolonging pain.

A gentle smile,

A caring conversation,

A Soothing platter sliding down the throat,

A glass of wine,

Complimented with your words in my ears.

- Date

All women are exotic,

All women are enigmatic,

All women can become *"Joker on LSD overdose"*,

You don't have to be a batman and stop her madness, because

"Madness, as you know is a lot like gravity,

All it takes is a little push."

                          - Don't Push.

Men are simple beings,

If you love them,

They will love you back,

Problem arises from what a man
contemplates as love.

Each man grew learning his own way to love
others,

For some men, Love can be more
complicated than any women,

For some men, love must be given to him
without any expectation for returns,

For some men, love is giving you more than
what you ever need,

Choose the one which suits you.

Just don't blame men for being himself.

- Men & Love.

There is no wrong in falling for an enigma,

One which makes you work for your love,

One that keeps you tip toeing around landmines.

Most times it will be a waiting game and a sport of persistence,

But for when the enigma understands that you are never going to leave him/her.

He/she will reward you more than what you ever asked for,

For he/she knows you are "*worthy*".

- Love (Difficulty: Very Hard).

Being called your name by that someone,

Actually not even your name, but a special name,

Being with that someone,

Doing silly something with that someone,

Sharing memories and scars with that someone,

That's what friendship is all about.

You can go crazy or have a curfew,

"They will be like water to your fountain."

- Friend.

As you carelessly sleep hearing my heart singing you lullaby,

I'm speechless how I ever got this close to you.

What did I ever do to deserve you?

- Dad.

It's hard to commit to someone who plays with the other,

A game of catch & throw with my heart.

As you always fling it up,

 I'm terrified whether you will catch it back?

Or should I catch it for myself?

All the while I'm caring your heart that's with me.

Aren't you worried?

Why are you acting as if the heart that I have is just a fake.

- Heartless?

You & I built an invisible bridge,

A bridge to cross our differences,

A bridge that connects the real us,

Why are you trying to burn the bridge?

Am I not worthy to connecting with?

Have our bridge turned from invisible to nothing for you?

As the distance grew greater,

Has my cry not reached you?

- Burning Bridges.

Most couple go out of their ways,

Turning the once shrine, that they spent
building brick by brick.

Into instant ruins.

Then they blame it on *"Meant to be"*.

                              - Cowards.

Love is a paradox,

A paradox with two un-parallel combinations,

1. To love,

2. To be loved.

Destruction comes,

When one forgets to love oneself,

Before expecting to be loved by another.

- Love yourself first.

Dear god,

Why… Why am I spending too much time to come up with love poems?

What's the need for every poem to be about "*love*"?

Why do people "*love*" it so much?

- (Love)ception.

Some know themselves, that they are "Monsters".

A sentient that exactly knows how much pain it can cause.

They usually push away those who love them,

Like a deteriorating grenade with empathy,

They simply don't want to cause collateral damage,

When they eventually explode.

It's their way of saying "*I love you*".

- Reluctant lover.

"Your *actions say more than your words do*"

That just a lame way of saying,

"You are full of shit."

                       - No nonsense Philosophy.

Love has the ability to turn you into a broken player,

Mindlessly looping the same thing over and over.

- That name and face.

Every now and then,

You look back at your choices,

It's mostly *"Why was I that stupid?"*

- Teenage Memories.

Some relationship is like looking at a mirror and punching it,

You don't just hurt yourself,

But you'll lose sight of yourself in the process.

As you spend countless days,

Searching for yourself in the leftover broken pieces,

You may never see through what is broken.

- Move on.

Wanting is a witch,

It will most probably trick you,

Convince you to accept hell saying "*It will be heaven*".

- Bad choices.

Some people expect only "LA" from others,

But each person is a road map,

Filled with,

Terrific cities and boring counties,

Twisty curves and empty stretches,

Hills and plateaus.

If you don't want a journey,

Don't bother me.

                              - Find somebody else.

I'm struggling,

Struggling to make words,

Struggling to make something meaningful,

Struggling to make it worthwhile,

Every day I'm failing.

- Failing Forward.

Some access,

Not to own,

But to sample.

Each takes huge chunks,

Leaving nothing to own.

                    - Used.

Some fill love onto people who can't carry.

Leaving some,

To think themselves as "*unwanted*".

- Deservers of love.

You are an island,

If he/she doesn't find you adventurous,

Then throw him/her onto a boat,

KICK THEM OUT.

- No place for such.

When he/she treat you kinder than you
ever wanted,

Adores your every actions,

He/she doesn't want to just grab your
attention,

He/she wants you.

- Crush.

Snakes shed skin,

Lizards severs tail,

Children lose teeth,

Adults shed tears.

Everything for everybody else comes back
new & improved day by day,

Ironically,

For the adults, only the tear collections
grow day by day.

                          - Collectors.

I'm guitar,

I needed to be learnt,

I needed to be stringed now and then,

But you wanted garageband.

- Old soul.

Some generics,

Finds a bewildered beast,

A being with raw emotions & uncontained
rage for life,

Befriends them, make them fall under.

Then in the name of *"commitment"*,

Puts them in a zoo called *"Relationship"*.

- Beast gone rogue.

It's a pity,

Forgetting your face and voice,

While feelings still linger on.

There is something I cannot put my finger on.

Oh, what have you done to me?

- My dear sin.

I can't curse you,

I can't wish you bad luck,

I can't blame you for everything.

As our love chokes me to death,

I'm just trying to breathe.

- Post-trauma.

We keep trading punches,

As neither want to embrace each other,

We are simply knocking ourselves to a hug.

Only to rest and resume.

In this endless bout,

We are hanging together by the *love thread*.

- Love Tournament.

You fell into a clear pond.

Don't leave it when it gotten mirky,

Especially when it is you who caused it.

- Give Closure.

No matter the remedy,

For what is broken, Stays broke.

No amount of piecing together will make
the cracks vanish.

- Shattered.

One vs one,

A game being played for many lifetimes,

Infinite strategies and possibilities,

Endless maps and NPCs,

Where commitment & cheating are main options,

That decides how it ends.

Few rematches work, many needs reboot.

- Love.

I'm yours,

You may want me to wash away,

But I'm like the beach sand,

I'll be all over you even before you notice.

- Too affectionate.

Woke up,

As the sun glaring red through my eyelids.

I kept my eyes shut,

Troubled & annoyed that I couldn't find your hands,

To pull them over my head.

Then all of a sudden,

You covered my eyes,

Elbowing over my forehead.

How are you this attentive even as you sleep?

- My mindreader.

We started as friends,

Then we played with the thought of being more,

Fortunately, that thought became reality,

Unfortunately,

It was a reality only for me.

- Waiting.

Our life is a conundrum,

More and more people will come and go,

Even the people who you want to stay,

Will eventually disappear.

Like water -> steam -> nothing.

You may try stopping them,

But it will be like,

Trying to hold water with your hands stretched out.

Fortunately, they will remain as a memory & moisture on your mind & hand.

> \- Let them go.

For all those who think of me as *"nothing"*.

I'm the wind,

I'll pass around you without you even
noticing,

Or

I'll blow you away like a trash-bag stuck in a
hurricane.

*I'm walking away because you don't
deserve my wrath.*

- Odd one out.

Some rarely grow up,

Especially, when it comes to showing love.

They will become a child needing for attention,

They will go crazy,

They will hurt themselves.

They want your attention.

No, they need your attention.

So they can feel special.

They aren't jealous,

They just want to be loved.

                                        - Pursuit for love.

Isn't it sad?

When the person whom you known,

In their flesh and blood,

In their laugh and voice,

In their anger and smile,

In their face and body.

Suddenly just isn't there anymore.

Someone who was tangible and real,

Vanished.

Left to be nothing but a corpse,

A mere shell for their existence.

Where did they go?

&

Why can't we accept them being gone?

- Bless their soul.

They have been the carriers of people's tears,

They were the one, who listened.

They were the one, who got drenched.

But still feel more comforting than any person.

A clothed companion.

- Pillow.

Most of the time,

I'm just overwhelmed.

By all the pain I'm going through.

By every disappointment I'm enduring.

By the poor state of living, which somehow feels far worse than I could ever consider as "*acceptable*".

By choices and consequences, which I have not contributed to.

I'm just in constant madness over the results I wasn't responsible for.

- Underprivileged.

I never write to satisfy people,

I never write to make perfect sense,

I never write because I'm full of love,

I never write for self – satisfaction,

I write to escape the everlasting emptiness.

One that is crippling my mind, day and night.

I'm just a guy trying to fill my infinite void.

Struggling to make my solitude, a survival.

- Sociopath's strategy.

Imagine a leaf,

Once nothing,

Turned into a sprout,

Then gradually grows from green to brown.

Decaying during the process.

Designated to fall as one among many,

Only to be swept away,

Like it's all for nothing.

Now, look at yourself.

                    - Make it worthwhile.

"Heart wants what it wants"

Said by not a single Heart patient ever.

- It's just a blood pump.

Pain is a pick axe,

Agony is a sanding paper,

Resulting experience is a novelty art,

An exhibit that can mean as common or as desirable,

Depending on the audience.

- Surround yourself with good audience.

From one sociopath to another or to anyone,

Being alone is exhausting.

Us being easily bored, doesn't help us either.

Isolation has its borders,

We are just *"immigrants",* whom are camped at the border for a long time.

Because we, sociopath have so much more to give,

But never given a chance.

We just had been left out.

First by choice, then by judgement.

We grew distant not because we wanted to,

We grew distant because we were forced to.

- We are a wasted opportunity.

Ying and yang,

Lock and key,

Love and hate,

Success and failure,

Yes and no,

Men and women.

There is no equal ground is there?

Why is it always a co-op?

                    - stuck in solo.

Rats are around 95% genetically identical to us,

We are more or less just 5% better than something that is tiny,

On the upside, we all have similar basic structure,

It's just the wiring, coding, skins and inventory that differs us from one another.

- Just nerding out.

You'll get numb,

You'll get used to,

You won't be offended anymore,

You will lose grip of the status quo,

You will see through what's made up and
what's real,

You will start to live only for yourself.

                      - Unfortunate but necessary.

There are two sides to the coin.

One which

"You & your beliefs are real",

Another which

"You & yourself is a fake".

                     - Pick a side & stick with it.

Waiting for receiving a "*I'm sorry*" is similar to saving up,

You'll probably need it very rarely,

But it's good to have it.

For a silly satisfaction or a prolonging pain.

                    - We are stupid sometimes.

In love, both men and women are like a *"runner up award"*.

You spend a lot of time & effort yearning for it,

But you may never get the satisfaction out of it.

There must always be this endless competition of winning over the other.

For that suffering itself is a prize,

Which only you and your significant other,

Can value and understand.

                              - Work for it.

There is this great power,

A kind of power only the forgiving people will know and understand.

The power of knowing each person's sin,

The power of knowing those sin's eventual ultimatum,

The power of keeping tabs on those sinners,

The power of waiting till they destroy themselves,

Just to lend them a hand when they are down and say "*Bless you*".

It is the spell that will save them,

When everything they were once proud of becomes their death sentence.

- The power of kindness.

You must be a grain of salt on a pepper pot,

You must surround yourself with those who know and understand,

That you are very vulnerable and fragile,

That you are a different kind of something else.

That you are a special specimen,

One who lives and breathe in the same air as them.

- Cherished circle.

We dwell on our *"past"*,

We dread on our *"future"*,

We tear for the once troubled times,

We fear for the unknown and what ifs,

All of which suffocates life out of our *"present"*.

- Don't die today itself.

Ever wondered,

That you are nothing but full of natural fibres called "*muscles*",

That you are nothing but full of liquid called "*blood*",

That your breath is nothing but a by-product of a fleshy porous bag called "*Lungs*",

That your life is nothing but a mystery with only one possible ending,

That you are nothing but a ridiculously random collection of other people's DNA leftovers.

Can't you see..?

You are a miracle. You are the stuff of magic.

- You.

Women's lives are a battleground,

A place where men compete to take control.

                          - Sad but true.

Try to fit in,

It's like a wedge under your boulder,

But when the wedge deteriorate,

Roll down, squashing everything on your path,

For you, a meteor which averted to apathy,

Destined to demolish whatever that stops you.

                          - Meteor ascension.

We are forced,

Forced to accept certain templates over the natural creativity,

Forced to accept the certain skins over the endless palette,

Forced to defend what we were forced to accept.

Forced to exile if when we wakeup & rebel against it.

- Social belief system.

We seldom talk about sex sociably,

Like it's not part of who we are.

Why is it such a taboo?

It is as if we all never practice it for ourselves.

                    - What's wrong with people?

Just because someone blind thrown you away,

Doesn't make you less valuable,

You are a diamond,

Raise your price

&

Find your way back into the store.

- Connoisseurs are waiting.

These days the concept of *"Beauty"* is put forward

by

Empty people

with

Shallow life.

         - Unfortunate turn of events.

I among most people,

Fool myself saying *"I'm happy"*,

While I'm roasting in hell.

- Doomed.

For there is endless night,

There will definitely be a dawn.

No matter how little it may last,

Cull yourself for those little fleeting moments of sunshine.

- Worth waiting.

For those who are wondering,

I'm an Indian,

My native is Tamil,

For me, English is as foreign as I am to you.

Yet here we are sharing time together.

As of this moment, I'm a nobody who became somebody on your conscience.

With me and my words serving you and your time.

A prey for your mind.

A feast for your eyes.

                                        - Dear you.

We struggle so much,

With all the need and greed,

With all the earnings and expenses,

With all the time and effort for a degree,

With all the melancholy over finding &
forlonging a job.

But at the end of the day,

We are nothing more than "*what & who we
love*" and "*what & who loves us*".

                                        - Life.

Giving doesn't need to be returned.

As you give only what you can afford to give,

Giving can itself be a reward.

Especially when you are giving to someone who can't ever possibly give anything back to you.

It's the way of keeping hope alive in our wrath wreaking world.

- Give.

Hello,

I hope you had a good time.

It really means a lot to me that you found my book worthy of your time.

Do leave your honest thoughts about the book.

Your reviews will be a great deal of help to me.

Recommend the book to your beloved friends as well.

You can check out my other books by visiting my author page on amazon.

If you want to express yourself to me personally,

You are always welcome to reach me via e-mail.
My mail id is balashiva2796@gmail.com
Or
Tweet me @ibalashiva

If you loved this book so much & you want to buy me a beverage or grab me a bite to show your support,
Paypal me using balashiva2796@gmail.com

Thank you ever so much.

Made in the USA
Middletown, DE
11 March 2019